# I Wish I Had Glasses Like Rosa
## Quisiera tener lentes como Rosa

Written by / Escrito por Kathryn Heling and Deborah Hembrook
Illustrated by / Ilustrado por Bonnie Adamson
Translated by / Traducido por Eida de la Vega

*To all my little kindergarten friends with glasses, especially Kat!*
*— Love from Mrs. Hembrook*
*XO*

*To Joshua and Amy, best friends!*
*— KEH*

*To Jenny and Steffie, always, glasses or not!*
*— BCA*

Text Copyright ©2007 by Kathryn Heling and Deborah Hembrook
Illustration Copyright ©2007 by Bonnie Adamson
Translation Copyright ©2007 by Raven Tree Press

Heling, Kathryn and Hembrook, Deborah.

I wish I had glasses like Rosa/written by Kathryn Heling and Deborah Hembrook; illustrated by Bonnie Adamson; translated by Eida de la Vega = Quisiera tener lentes como Rosa/escrito por Kathryn Heling and Deborah Hembrook; ilustrado por Bonnie Adamson; traducción al español de Eida de la Vega.–1ˢᵗ ed.–McHenry, IL: Raven Tree Press, 2007.

p.; cm.

Text in English and Spanish.

Summary: Abby goes to elaborate and comical lengths to get glasses like Rosa. She realizes she might have something that is just as desirable as the longed-for glasses. Abby gains appreciation of her own uniqueness.

ISBN-10–0-9724973-7-4  hardcover
ISBN-13–978-0-9724973-7-4

ISBN 10–0-9770906-5-5 paperback
ISBN 13–978-0-9770906-5-5

1. Eyeglasses–Juvenile Fiction. 2. Individuality–Juvenile Fiction. 3. Self Esteem–Juvenile Fiction.  4. Bilingual books–English and Spanish 5. [Spanish language materials–books.] I. Hembrook, Deborah. II. Adamson, Bonnie, ill. III. Vega, Eida de la. IV. Title. V. Title: Quisiera tener lentes como Rosa.

PZ73.H38345 2007

LCCN–2006933678

[E]–dc22

CIP

Printed in China
10 9 8 7 6 5 4 3 2 1
first edition

# I Wish I Had Glasses Like Rosa
## Quisiera tener lentes como Rosa

Written by / Escrito por Kathryn Heling and Deborah Hembrook

Illustrated by / Ilustrado por Bonnie Adamson

Translated by / Traducido por Eida de la Vega

Raven Tree Press
A DIVISION OF DELTA SYSTEMS CO., INC.

I wish I had glasses like Rosa.
They make her look beautiful!

Quisiera tener lentes como Rosa.
¡Se ve muy bonita con ellos!

4

Rosa and I like to build.
We wear safety glasses.
I love wearing glasses!

A Rosa y a mí nos gusta construir cosas.
Usamos gafas de protección.
¡Me encanta usar gafas!

One morning, I wore my grandma's reading glasses.
Everything looked funny.

Una mañana, me puse los lentes de leer de mi abuela.
Todo se veía rarísimo.

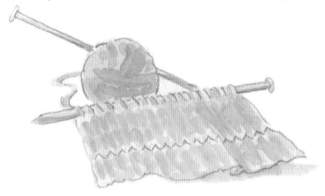

Then they slipped off my nose.
I'll never do that again!

Se me deslizaban por la nariz.
¡No lo volveré a hacer!

When I swim, I wear goggles.
I pretend they're real glasses.

Cuando nado, uso anteojos
y me hago la idea de que son lentes de verdad.

I wear them on the beach, too.

También me los dejo puestos
cuando me siento en la arena.

16

In art class, I made glasses out of clay.
They were perfect.

En la clase de arte, hice unos lentes de plastilina.
Me quedaron perfectos.

Then they drooped.
I'll never do that again!

Pero se me aflojaron enseguida.
¡No lo volveré a hacer!

I found the glasses my dad wore for a party.

Encontré los lentes que mi papá usó en una fiesta.

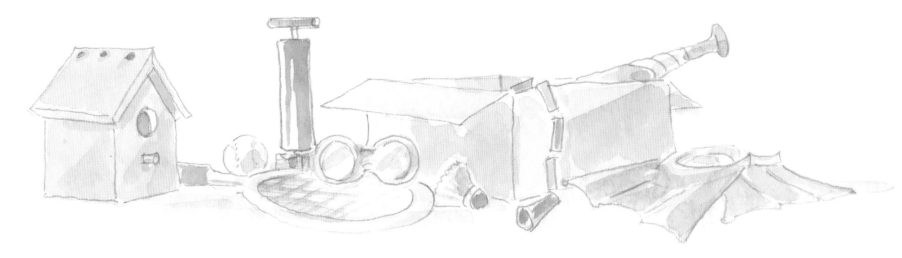

They made my nose itch.
Dad said I needed a shave.

Pero me hacían cosquillas en la nariz.
Papá dijo que me vendría bien un afeitado.

At recess, I wore my eyeball glasses.

En el recreo, usé unos lentes con los ojos colgando.

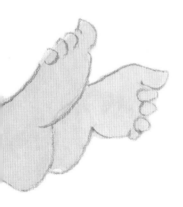

The eyeballs bounced when I jumped rope.
I'll never do that again!

Los ojos daban brincos cada vez que yo saltaba la suiza.
¡No lo volveré a hacer!

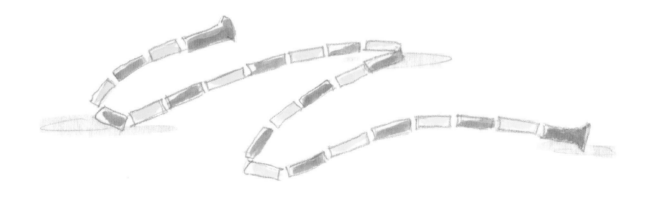

27

I still wish I had glasses
like Rosa!
But Rosa wishes she had
freckles like me!

Todavía quiero tener lentes
como Rosa.
¡Sin embargo, Rosa quiere
tener pecas como yo!

28

Imagine that!

¡Imagínate!

# Vocabulary
## English

glasses
beautiful
nose
swim
beach
art class
Dad
party
jump
imagine

# Vocabulario
## Español

los lentes, las gafas
bonita
la nariz
nado (nadar)
la arena
la clase de arte
el papá
la fiesta
saltaba (saltar)
imagínate (imaginar)